Marcel is a French mouse. He lives on a beautiful old
boat in Paris. (His home is under the kitchen floor.) He
likes books, restaurants and old films. He likes the
opera, too.

One evening in June, Marcel finishes a detective story.
Then he goes to have dinner with some friends. They
live in the metro station at the *Louvre*.

1

After dinner, Marcel waits at the station. He sees two men standing next to him. The tall one is reading a magazine, "Look," he says, "here she is: '*Opera star Miss Zaza Dupont with her beautiful one million pound diamond ring – the White Star.*'"

"'*Her*' beautiful diamond ring?" The short man looks at the photo and laughs. "Not after tonight," he says.

Marcel's mouth opens. "What?! Are the men going to *steal* Zaza Dupont's diamond?"

He remembers an evening at the opera two weeks before. Zaza's green dress. The music. The beautiful White Star on her finger. No! They *can't* steal it!

The train comes and the men get on. Marcel pulls down his hat and follows them.

Half an hour later he gets off again at *La Mouette* station. But there are hundreds of people, and Marcel loses the two men. Then he sees an old mouse. "Excuse me," he says. "Do you know where Zaza Dupont lives?" But when Marcel finds Zaza's house, it is too late. "Yes – two men," she is telling the police on the telephone. "And they've got the White Star."

At that moment Marcel hears a motor start. "Where's that coming from?" he thinks. Then he sees something at the end of the road. It's them! It's the thieves and they're stealing a car! He runs across Zaza's garden and down the street. He can see the car's number-plate. It's near. Very near. "Can I . . .?" he thinks, and he jumps.

Yes!! Marcel sits on the number-plate. "Good," he thinks. Then, after a second or two . . . "But what happens now?"

The thieves drive across Paris very fast. Marcel can hear them in the car. They are laughing and talking. But Marcel is not laughing. He is very, *very* angry. After half an hour the car stops next to a café.

It is late and the café is quiet. In one corner there is a woman. The thieves sit at her table. Marcel sits *under* the table and listens. "Have you got it?" the woman asks. The tall man takes a box from his jacket. Then he opens it. "Look," he says. "Ahhh!" The woman puts a hand to her mouth. "What a *beautiful* diamond!" "This is it," thinks Marcel. "This is the moment."

He bites the tall man's leg very hard. "Aiiieee!" The tall
man throws up his arms. The box and the White Star
fly across the room. "What's that on the floor?" one
waiter asks. "I don't know," says another. "Is it . . .? No,
it can't be a diam . . ." But before he can finish, Marcel
runs across the room. He puts the White Star around
his neck. Then he runs to the door.

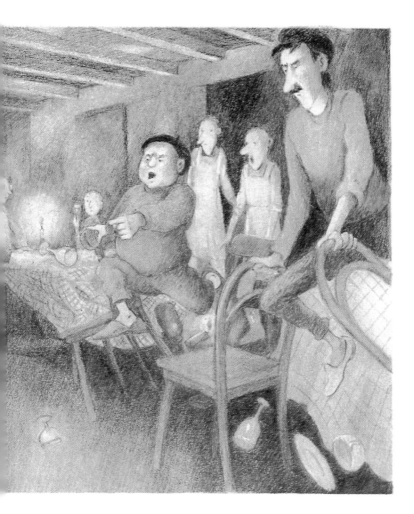

The thieves jump up and follow him. Suddenly there
are tables and chairs everywhere. "What's happening?"
an old man asks. "I don't know," his wife answers.
"Who can understand young people these days?"
"Stop that mouse!" says the tall man. "Shut the door!"
says the short one. But they are too late. Marcel runs
out of the café and does not look back.

After ten minutes he stops. There is nobody following him, but . . . where is he? Marcel looks right and left. Then he sees a big, white church. "Ah! – the Sacré Coeur," he thinks. "Now I know where I am."

It is late and there are no metro trains, but Marcel is not tired. He walks back to Zaza's house. When he gets there, she is asleep in bed.

There is a table next to the window. On it Marcel can see lots of photographs, boxes and perfume bottles. He runs across the floor and up one leg of the table. "Now…" he thinks, "…it's time to take off the White Star. In the morning Zaza is going to be very…" Then Marcel stops. Oh, no! He cannot take the ring off. He pulls and pulls, but nothing happens.

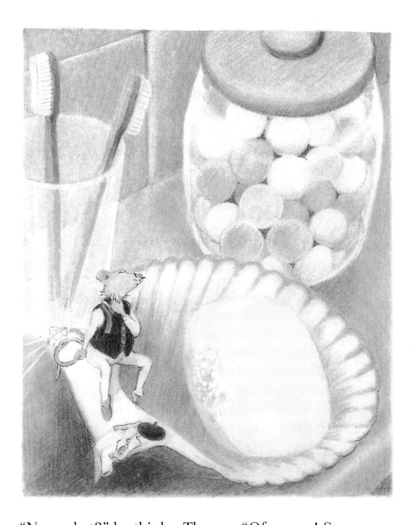

"Now what?" he thinks. Then ... "Of course! Some soap!" He runs down the table leg and across the floor. Zaza's bathroom door is open. Marcel goes in and looks up. A soap-dish is above his head.

Ten seconds later he is sitting in it. He puts some soap on his neck. Then he closes his eyes and pulls again. *Yes*! This time the diamond ring comes off.

In the morning Zaza finds the White Star. It is on her
bedroom table between two perfume bottles. "But . . . I
don't understand," she says. "Thieves don't bring
things back. How . . . ?" She looks at the ring. Then she
looks at her face in the mirror. Then she looks at the
ring again. "And why is there soap on it?" She
telephones the police.

Next day, Zaza's story is in all the newspapers.

'OPERA STAR'S £1,000,000 RING IS SAFE' says one.

'THIEVES BRING BACK DUPONT DIAMOND' says another.

'NOW POLICE ASK, "WHY?" '

And there are lots of photos of Zaza with the White
Star. At home. At the opera house. Standing in front of
the Eiffel Tower. She looks very happy in all of them.

Marcel is happy, too. Back on his boat he reads the
newspaper stories. Then he looks in the mirror. There
is a thin, red line on his neck. "What a night!" he says.
After that, he washes, has breakfast and opens the
window. It is beautiful, warm morning. Marcel looks
up at the blue sky and smiles. "Now . . ." he thinks,
"what's going to happen today?"

ACTIVITIES

Pages 1–7

Before you read

1 Read the Word List at the back of the book. What are the twenty words in your language? Find them in a dictionary.

2 Look at the pictures in the book and answer the questions.

    a Does Marcel live in a house or on an old boat?

    b On page 2, who is Marcel looking at?

    c What is on the right hand of the woman on page 3?

    d Who has got it on page 7?

While you read

3 Are the sentences right (✓) or wrong (✗)?

    a Marcel lives on a beautiful old boat in London.   .....

    b Zaza Dupont is an opera star.   .....

    c Marcel gets on a train at La Mouette.   .....

    d He gets off the train at the Louvre.   .....

    e The thieves steal Zaza's diamond ring.   .....

    f She telephones Marcel.   .....

    g The thieves steal a black car.   .....

    h They go to a cinema.   .....

After you read

4 Work with a friend. You are the thieves in the black car.

    What do you say about the White Star?

    How much money can you get for it?

    What can you do with the money?

Pages 8–15

Before you read

5 Look at the pictures. What do you think?

   a How does Marcel get the diamond ring?

   b Where does he take the ring to?

   c Does Zaza know about Marcel?

While you read

6 Finish the sentences.

   a Marcel puts the White Star around his ....

   b He takes the diamond to Zaza Dupont's ....

   c It's very late and Zaza is in ....

   d First, Marcel can't get the ring .... his neck.

   e In the morning Zaza .... her ring.

   f After that, her story is in all the ....

   g Zaza and the .... don't know about Marcel.

   h Zaza is happy and Marcel is .... too.

After you read

7 Look at pages 8–9. You are in the Café Flo. You are talking to a friend on your phone. Suddenly, two men are running across the room! What are they doing? What can you see and hear? Talk to your friend about it.

8 A diamond ring, a black car and some soap are important in the story. Why? Write your answers.

9 Write about the people in the story.

   a Zaza   **b** the two thieves   **c** Marcel

WORD LIST *with example sentences*

around (prep) There are eight chairs *around* the table.

bathroom (n) Wash your hands in the *bathroom*.

bite (v) Don't put your hand near that animal! It *bites* people!

box (n) She doesn't like banks. She puts her money in a *box* under the bed.

café (n) Let's go to the *café* and have some coffee.

diamond (n) *Diamonds* are very small, very expensive, and women love them.

dinner (n) We usually eat *dinner* at 8 o'clock in the evening.

finger (n) You have five *fingers* on your hand.

follow (v) That man is always behind us. He's *following* us.

jump (v) The children are running and *jumping* into the river.

mouse (n) Marcel is a brown *mouse*. Some *mice* are white.

neck (n) This animal has a small head on a long *neck*.

number-plate (n) Every car has two *number-plates* with letters and numbers on them.

opera (n) The music from Mozart's *operas* is very famous.

pull (v) He's very strong. He can *pull* a big car behind him.

ring (n) She has an expensive *ring* on her finger.

soap (n) Wash your hands with *soap* and water.

star (n) At night, I go into the garden and look up at the *stars*.
Tom Cruise and Julia Roberts are famous film *stars*.

steal (v) He *steals* money from old people, and the police are looking for him.

thief (n) This *thief* steals cars. There are many car *thieves* in the town.